CHRISTMAS!

NORTH POLE

By Michael Garland

SCHOLASTIC PRESS / NEW YORK

"Ho! Ho! Ho! Oh, what a Christmas!"

Everything started off the same magical way Christmas always does. Santa and his reindeer took off from the North Pole, loaded with presents for all the boys and girls around the world.

"Now, Dasher! Now, Dancer! Now, Prancer and Vixen! On, Comet! On, Cupid! On, Donner and Blitzen!" Santa called out as the sleigh raced across the starry sky.

Then **POP! RIP! S-T-R-E-T-C-H!**
The harness that attached the reindeer to Santa's sleigh was tearing.
With one final **BOING!** it snapped in two!
"Ho! Ho! — oh, no!"

The reindeer streaked off into the night, and
Santa and his sleigh headed back down to earth like
a BIG, FAT, JOLLY RED SKYROCKET!

A snow-covered mountain rose up from the
north woods. The sleigh struck the snowy peak, then
skidded and slid and slipped and spun down the
slope.

Now the sleigh was going so fast, Santa couldn't stop it! A great plume of snow flew high up in the air as the sleigh tore across a field.

"Ho! Ho! Slow!" Santa howled, right before he crashed KABLAMM! into the side of a barn.

Santa wasn't hurt. He just sat there, brushing the snow off and wondering what to do now.

The barn door creaked open, and a sleepy sheep peeked out.

"Ho, ho . . . oh, hello," said Santa.

The sheep stepped out into the snow, followed by another sheep, then a horse, then two cows, then a goat, then a pig, and finally a very old dog. "Well, this is a fine mess." Santa's belly jiggled as he laughed. "Those reindeer must be halfway across the world by now!"

"I can't disappoint all those children!" Santa said. "I *have* to get them their presents!"

Santa was thinking. Suddenly he smiled, and with a twinkle in his eye he said, "Maybe *you* can help me?"

Santa turned the sleigh right side up. And with a little help from his new friends, all the presents were packed onto the sleigh.

Then Santa lined up all the animals, two by two, in front of the sleigh.

Santa wiggled his nose, snapped his fingers, and POOF!
In one instant FLASH! they were all attached to the sleigh with a
beautiful new harness.

Santa sprang to his sleigh with a quick little whistle. "Giddyup!"
And before the animals knew it, **UP** they went! They were flying!
"Now, Sheep! Now, Goat! Now, Piggy and Cows! On, Horsey! On,
Doggie! Oh, what a Christmas flight we have now!"
The once silent night was filled with mooing and barking
and baaing and neighing and oink, oink, oinking!

As they approached the first house, Santa called, "Ho! Ho! Whoa! Whoa! Whoooaaaa!"

They landed with a big THUD! STOMP! THWACK! WHUMP! and WHINNY! Then they screeched to a halt just at the edge of the roof.

"Not *too* bad for your first time," said Santa as he slipped down the chimney.

Delivering presents to all the children of the world is a big job to do in one night. They were so far behind schedule! They had to work twice as hard! There was barely time for cookies and milk this year!

One country after another, one house after another, one present after another — they finally finished as the morning sun came over the horizon. Santa was covered in ashes and soot, and the animals were all so hungry! "Ho, ho, home," said Santa with a big yawn and stretch. "You did a great job. Now it's time to get you back to the barn."

The reindeer were waiting as Santa and his new team touched down.

"Ho! Ho! Ho! Oh, what a Christmas!" said Santa to the proud little band from the barn. "I couldn't have done it without you!"

Santa let out a big belly laugh as he took his new friends out of the harness and buckled his sheepish reindeer in.

"I've left you a special surprise in the barn," said Santa with a smile. Then he hopped up on his sleigh, and with a flick of the reins he headed back to the North Pole.

Over his shoulder, he shouted out to his new friends, "Ho! Ho! Ho! Merry Christmas!"

To Winnie Whipple, my first Scholastic art director.
— MG

Library of Congress Cataloging-in-Publication Data
Garland, Michael, 1952–
Oh, what a Christmas! / by Michael Garland.
p. cm.
Summary: After Santa loses his reindeer midflight on Christmas Eve, he improvises by seeking the help of some barnyard animals to complete his trip.
ISBN 978-0-545-24210-3 (hardcover)
[1. Christmas—Fiction. 2. Santa Claus—Fiction. 3. Domestic animals—Fiction. 4. Humorous stories.] I. Title.
PZ7.G18413Oh 2011
[E]—dc22
2011005284

10 9 8 7 6 5 4 3 2 1   11 12 13 14 15
Printed in Singapore   46
First edition, September 2011